Blast to the Past

Blast to the Past®

⑦ Washington's War

By Stacia Deutsch & Rhody Cohon

Illustrated by Guy Francis

ALADDIN PAPERBACKS

New York   London   Toronto   Sydney

To my friends who held my hands: Robin Abrams,
Erika Frady, Yanina Feinerman, and Annie Zeigon.
With special love to Leah Hochman, who made me eat
fish. And as always, to Rhody, who wouldn't let me quit.
—Stacia

To Mom and Dad. Thank you.
—Rhody

ALADDIN PAPERBACKS
An imprint of Simon & Schuster Children's Publishing Division
1230 Avenue of the Americas, New York, NY 10020
Text copyright © 2007 by Stacia Deutsch and Rhody Cohon
Illustrations copyright © 2007 by Guy Francis
All rights reserved, including the right of
reproduction in whole or in part in any form.
BLAST TO THE PAST is a registered trademark of Stacia Deutsch and Rhody Cohon.
ALADDIN PAPERBACKS and colophon are trademarks of Simon & Schuster, Inc.
Designed by Lisa Vega
The text of this book was set in Minion.
Manufactured in the United States of America
First Aladdin Paperbacks edition January 2007
2 4 6 8 10 9 7 5 3 1
The Library of Congress Control Number: 2006927768
ISBN-13: 978-1-4169-3390-8
ISBN-10: 1-4169-3390-5

Contents

PROLOGUE
Time Travel

IF YOU SAID TO ME, "HEY, ABIGAIL! WHAT'S YOUR favorite thing in the whole world?" I would have to answer, "History Club."

History Club is way better than playing video games. Better than riding my bike. Even better than eating pizza with pineapple and olives.

After school on Mondays, our third-grade social studies teacher, Mr. Caruthers, sends three of my friends and me on a mission back in time. Jacob, his twin brother Zack, Bo, and I call our top secret time-travel adventures History Club.

And our teacher, Mr. Caruthers, is so supercool, we call him Mr. C.

One day, a woman named Babs Magee stole a

time-travel computer that Mr. C invented in his laboratory under the school gym. Now she's popping around history, visiting important people on a list of names that Mr. C made.

Babs Magee wants to be famous. But she doesn't want to work for it. She'd rather steal other people's inventions or ideas.

It's a lame way to get famous.

When Mr. C discovered what Babs Magee was doing, he knew he needed to keep history straight. Since he is too busy working on a new invention, he asked Bo, Jacob, Zack, and me to help him out. It's our job to go back in time and convince those famous Americans not to give up their dreams.

Mr. C gave us a brand-new time-travel computer. It looks like a handheld video game with a larger screen and extra buttons. When we put a special cartridge in the back, a glowing green hole opens and we jump through time. Taking the cartridge out brings us home again.

We have two hours to get the task done. So far, we've been really lucky. On all our adventures,

Jacob, Zack, Bo, and I have managed to keep history on track. We've foiled Babs Magee's schemes, and landed back at school with seconds to spare.

Today is Monday. I can hardly wait for school to end and History Club to begin.

CHAPTER ONE
Monday

When I entered the classroom, Maxine Wilson was already sitting at her table.

"Hey, Abigail," she greeted me, like always. I've been friends with Maxine since kindergarten. She's an awesome person and she has a really awesome stopwatch.

"Are you ready?" I asked her.

"Ready, Freddy," Maxine replied. She held up her stopwatch and winked at me.

The school bell was the signal.

Brrring.

Maxine pressed the little black button on her watch. We all rushed to our seats and turned to stare at the classroom door. No one dared look away, not even for a second.

Maxine kept track of the time. "Five minutes." She began the countdown. "Four minutes and thirty seconds."

Maxine announced the time until there were only ten seconds left. The whole class always chanted the last ten seconds out loud together: "Ten. Nine. Eigh—"

The door swung open. Was it our favorite teacher, Mr. C? Could he be early for the first time all year? Nope.

"I had to make a pit stop on the way to class," Zack explained to everyone as he walked into the classroom.

"Sit down! Quick!" I told him. "Mr. C will be here in a few seconds."

"I've got plenty of time." Zack yawned as he dragged himself over to our table. Zack and I sat with Jacob and our new friend Bo. Bo's real name is Roberto Rodriguez.

"Four seconds," Maxine warned. Zack plopped into his chair and turned to face the door. "Three. Two. One. Zero." Just as Maxine clicked off her stopwatch, the classroom door swung open. This time, it really was our teacher.

"See?" Zack said, leaning over and whispering in my ear. "I told you I had plenty of time. I saw Mr. C in the hallway when I was headed to class. I rushed ahead to get here first and—"

"Be quiet." Jacob cut Zack off. "Mr. C's about to begin."

Zack snorted at his brother and challenged, "Make me."

Even though the boys were twins, they were as different as night and day.

Today Zack was wearing long pants that were torn in a hundred places. Different colored patches covered the rips. He had a sweatshirt on that looked like it was older than my great grandma. Breakfast stains were all over the sleeve. When it came to personality, Zack complained a lot and quit everything he tried. But he was totally funny and always came through when we needed him most.

Jacob, on the other hand, was neat and clean and focused on just one thing: computers. Today he was wearing a Hawaiian shirt, khaki pants, a leather belt, and a button that said, "West Hudson Elementary School Computer Club." Jacob was the Computer Club president.

Looking at the twins' snarly faces, I was afraid they might start to fight, but they both turned toward Mr. C as soon as he started talking.

"My apologies for being late," Mr. C said with a slight bow.

Every Monday was the same. Every Monday Mr. Caruthers was five minutes late. Every Monday he was wrinkled and messy. Only Jacob, Zack, Bo, and I knew the real reason why.

Mr. C never gave himself enough time on Mondays to make a time-travel cartridge for our History Club adventure and get to class on time, too. There was also a secret explosion that screwed up Mr. C's clothes and hair. It happened when he put the lid on the cartridge. Even though we've asked, Mr. C won't tell us why he doesn't just make the cartridge on Sundays. It sure would be easier. And he'd definitely be neater.

While Mr. Caruthers straightened his crumpled suit jacket, retied his bow tie, and combed his hair, Zack softly said to me, "Did you hear the joke about George—"

"Not now," I whispered back to Zack. "Mr. C is about to ask his 'what-if' question."

Mr. C finished straightening his clothes and leaned back on the edge of his desk. He was too cool to sit in a chair like other teachers.

"What if," he began, then paused. I sat up a little straighter.

Every Monday Mr. Caruthers asked us a new "what-if" question. He'd ask us to think about what the world would be like if someone famous gave up his or her dreams and quit. The discussion in class was always interesting and fun. But the best part was that whoever we talked about in class was the same person Zack, Jacob, Bo, and I would visit during History Club later.

I couldn't wait to hear who we'd be visiting today.

Mr. C leaned back farther on his desk. "What if—"

"Hey, Abigail," Zack poked me in the arm. "It's a

really good joke. Perfect for today! I heard it from two kids during my pit stop in the bathroom."

"Shhh," I hissed at Zack, and turned my attention back to Mr. C.

Zack poked me in the arm again. "Where did George Washington buy his ax?"

"I don't care," I replied, trying to hear what Mr. C was saying. I leaned forward, but all I could hear was Zack's soft giggling.

"At the chopping mall," Zack snickered. "That's a good one, eh?"

"No," I said, trying to keep my voice down. I usually think Zack is really funny, but the joke stunk. And his timing stunk too.

All around me hands were popping up in the air.

I couldn't believe it, Zack made me miss the "what-if" question! I always have good suggestions for the discussion. But now I had no idea who was going to quit. Or who we were visiting after school. Drat Zack and his stupid chopping joke.

Mr. C called on Ryota Yoshida. "Well," Ryota said confidently, "if he quit, there wouldn't be thirty-one

counties, seventeen cities, and one state named after him. That's for sure."

Anna Ramos didn't really answer the question. Instead she shared a few facts. Anna said he was married but never had children of his own. She also knew that he had lived in Virginia, New York, and Philadelphia, but never in the nation's capital.

I glanced over at Zack. Even though he'd ruined the question for me, maybe he knew who we were talking about. Besides, he was sitting closest to me at our table.

"Zack," I whispered, "do you know who we—," I began.

He interrupted me saying, "What would you get if you crossed George Washington with cattle feed?"

I shook my head. I didn't care about the answer to Zack's joke. I just wanted to know who we were talking about in class!

I totally refused to look at Zack anymore and leaned toward Jacob. He was listening to the other students and didn't notice me trying to catch his attention.

That left Bo. Bo reads a ton and knows everything about everything. He would totally know what was going on. I waved my hands trying to catch his eye.

Instead of getting Bo to look over at me, a horrible thing happened! Mr. C thought I wanted to be called on. "Abigail?" he asked me. "Do you have an idea what the world would be like if he quit?"

"I," I began, then stopped. I ran through the clues in my head. Nothing helped. I still didn't have any idea who we were talking about. I had two choices. One, tell Mr. C that I didn't know who we were discussing, or two, guess. I went for guessing.

"I suppose," I said, pretending I knew exactly what was going on, "that America wouldn't be the great country it is today." I hoped I didn't sound dumb.

"Very nice," Mr. C told me. I breathed a huge sigh of relief.

Then Mr. C asked Bo what he thought. Bo is very shy, especially around adults. He never volunteers to answer Mr. C's questions so Mr. C just calls on him.

"Well." Bo rubbed his chin as he talked. He did that when he was thinking really hard. "I suppose if he quit, America would have lost the Revolutionary War. We'd still be part of Britain. We certainly wouldn't have our own constitution since he helped write it. And—"

I knew I was so close to finding out who we were talking about. My heart began to beat faster. I scooted up to the very edge of my chair. My ears were prickling. I was ready to hear the rest of Bo's answer and find out the name. . . .

"And"—Bo paused a second, rubbing his chin even harder—"if he quit, he'd never have been the very first—"

Tap. Tap. Tap.

"What?!" I spun around to find Zack tapping on my shoulder. "Leave me alone." I quickly turned my head back to face Bo.

"But, Abigail," Zack whined, "don't you want to know the answer to the joke?"

I could see Bo's mouth moving, but because Zack was talking at the same time, I couldn't hear what Bo was saying.

Tap.

"WHAT?!" I snapped at Zack. Of course, I snapped in a whisper so we wouldn't get into trouble.

"The fodder of our country." Zack grinned widely. "That's the answer to the riddle." I stared at him blankly.

"Remember?" he said. "What do you get if you cross George Washington with animal feed?" He poked me in the arm. "The fodder of our country. Get it? Fodder is what farmers call hay and stuff like that like." Zack's belly was shaking with silent giggles. He had to hold on to the edge of his desk to keep from falling off his seat.

I turned away, totally annoyed.

When I finally caught up with the class discussion again, Mr. C was saying, "Good job, Bo. You have an excellent understanding of American history."

Just then, the bell rang. Class was over.

My favorite class was ruined.

I banged my head down on my desk with a crash.

CHAPTER TWO
Who?

I was mad at Zack. And I was embarrassed. I couldn't tell anyone that I didn't know who we'd talked about in social studies, especially since I'd answered a question about the mystery man, pretending I knew what was going on.

I would have to figure out who it was using detective skills. Good thing I am supercurious and like to ask questions. If I nosed around, no one would think it was different from any other day.

The first chance I had was a couple of hours later during recess. I found Cindy Cho on the playground near the slide.

"So," I said casually as I approached, "how'd you like Mr. C's class today?"

Cindy climbed up the slide as she answered. "I loved talking about him. I had no idea that he didn't wear a wig but put white powder in his hair instead." She zoomed down the slide, adding, "I also didn't know that his teeth were made of bone or ivory, not wood."

More interesting facts I'd missed in class. Double drat that Zack Osborne and his dopey jokes.

"And what about Mr. C's question?" I asked slyly. "What do you think the world would be like if *he* quit?" I hoped that Cindy hadn't answered the question in class. I didn't think Mr. C had called on her, but honestly, I was having a hard time remembering. I was going to have a serious talk with Zack when I got the chance.

"Oh," Cindy said before running off to the swings, "I thought the same as you!" And with that, she hustled away. No luck there.

In the hall on the way to math, I caught up with Juan Garcia standing by his locker.

"So," I said, leaning against the wall nearby, trying to look like I wasn't up to anything, "were

you surprised by Mr. C's 'what-if' question in class today?"

"No way," Juan replied. He took a few books out of his locker. "We were talking about the best military general in American history."

I nodded, acting like I knew exactly who Juan was talking about. Juan fake punched me in the shoulder and went to get a drink of water before the next class.

I was gathering more clues, but so far, I still didn't know who Jacob, Zack, Bo, and I were going to visit after school.

Before math class began, I took out a piece of blank paper and wrote down everything I knew: "Married." "Never lived in nation's capital." In parenthesis next to that I wrote "Washington, D.C.," because that's the nation's capital. "There are a lot of cities named after him. A state, too." "Powdered hair." "Ivory teeth." "Military general." "Lived during Revolutionary War." "Helped create the United States Constitution."

One or two more good clues and I could definitely solve this mystery.

During math class I sat between Noah Linkon and his cousin Devon. The Linkons were in Mr. C's social studies class too, but I didn't know either of them very well. They were assigned to a table across the room from me.

While we were waiting for our teacher to pass out the homework assignment, I whispered, "Have either of you been thinking about Mr. C's question from class today?"

"Nah," Devon said. "I was busy doing other stuff." He told me he'd played soccer at recess and his team had won against a group of fifth graders.

I wasn't really interested in talking about soccer, so I decided to turn to Noah instead. I asked, "Do you think there was anything more that Mr. C could have said about—" How was I going to phrase this? I paused to think before saying, "About *that* guy we talked about?"

I am pretty sure Noah immediately caught on that I didn't know who I was talking about, because he replied, "*That guy* changed the course of history." He obviously wasn't going to give up the name.

"Did you know that when *that guy* began his second term, he gave the shortest inaugural address in history. His first one was short too, but that second one, wow, it was only one hundred thirty-five words." He stopped, then added with a grin, "No one mentioned that fact in class, did they?"

I smiled like I was totally clued in. "You sure know a lot about *that guy*."

"Yep," he said. "I bet I know almost as much about *that guy* as Bo." We both laughed. No one on Earth could possible know as much about anything as Bo.

Our teacher finished handing out the homework and the final bell rang. Right before I left the room, Noah tugged on my sleeve. He winked and said, "Think about last names." I thought about his: Linkon. We'd already visited Abraham Lincoln.

"Did you ask Devon who their recess soccer goalie was?" Noah asked me. It was such a weird question.

"Dude," Devon chimed in as he gathered his books, "Shanika doesn't let anything get by her. She rocks."

"Your goalie is Shanika Washing—?" I began,

then stopped midthought. "Thanks," I said quickly, and rushed out of the room.

School was over. The Linkons had given me the last few clues I needed. I was pretty sure I'd solved the mystery but wanted to be certain.

I knew I had to get to our social studies classroom to meet the boys for History Club, but I wanted to check something out first. I hurried into the school library.

In the reference section, I grabbed a dictionary off the shelf. "Inaugural," I muttered to myself. Noah had mentioned *that guy*'s "second inaugural address." I was a pretty good actress because I didn't know what "inaugural" meant. I had just grinned and nodded.

"In." "Inane." "Inattentive." "Inaugural." I found it.

"Marking a beginning." Under the definition, the word was used in a sentence:

The president gave his inaugural address before he took office.

An inaugural address was a president's first speech, marking the beginning of his term. An inaugural address meant *that guy* was president of the United States. A second address meant he was president twice.

All the clues came together. I finally knew who we were visiting. Yippee!

I hustled out of the library and ran all the way to Mr. C's classroom for History Club. When I flung open the door, I couldn't believe my eyes!

The green time-travel hole was already open. Glowing smoke covered the floor. Three backpacks were resting in a corner. Jacob and Zack were gone.

Bo was standing at the very edge of the time-travel hole.

"You're leaving without me?!" I asked, mouth hanging open, totally stunned.

Bo blushed. He was clearly embarrassed and explained in a soft, pained voice. "Jacob didn't want to put the cartridge into the back of the computer. But Zack was worried. He kept complaining about how we weren't going to have enough time for the adventure. We waited as long as we could."

I couldn't believe it. The boys were going to time-travel without me!

It was Zack's fault that I missed the discussion in my favorite class. His fault that I'd had to play detective all day. And his fault that I'd almost missed time-traveling.

I grabbed Bo's hand. "Let's go. Zack is not getting away with this!"

The two of us jumped into the glowing green hole together.

CHAPTER THREE

Valley Forge

THE FIRST THING I DID WHEN I LANDED WAS LOOK for Zack. My blood was boiling. I needed to talk to him—now!

I dropped Bo's hand and started searching. We'd landed in a large farm field. There were bales of hay stacked in neat rows. The area was flat, but rolling hills surrounded us. Clusters of trees grew on the hills. Fresh white snow dusted the ground.

When a gust of freezing wind blew, I stuffed my hands under the bottom of my shirt to keep them warm. Suddenly I realized that in my rush to jump through the time-travel hole, I had forgotten to take off my backpack. I quickly pulled it off, shuffled my books to the side, and took out my jacket. It was a simple red raincoat, not great for a snowy day, but still warmer than hanging around in my turtleneck and jeans.

I was on the prowl for Zack. I looked right and saw nothing but sheep and horses in wide pens. When I turned left, there he was! Zack was hurrying across the farm field at top speed. He seemed to be chasing after three men.

I sped past Bo, who was busy zipping up the light-weight coat he was wearing.

I hustled past Jacob, who was checking the settings on the computer. I heard him say, "Valley Forge, Pennsylvania. February 16, 1778," as I rushed by.

I noticed that Jacob had a jacket on too. The boys must have brought coats, knowing it was going to be cold. That made me even madder at Zack. I hadn't known to bring a coat and might not have if I hadn't accidentally brought my backpack along.

"Zack," I called out, my fists shaking with rage. "I can't believe you left without me!"

He didn't hear me, or else he was ignoring me, because I heard him shout out to the men, "Hey, guys! Wait up!"

Since Zack is the fastest runner in the third grade, he actually caught up to the three men. They stopped to talk. Perfect. Now, I had him right where I wanted him!

Ignoring the men Zack was with, I tackled him.

"Oof," Zack exclaimed with surprise as he fell back into the snow. I stood over him, hands on my hips, breathing hard.

"What are you doing?!" Zack was shocked.

"I'm mad at you," I replied, narrowing my eyes and looking at him hard.

"We don't have time for this, Abigail," Zack insisted, struggling to get up. "They're going to get away! If they leave we won't have any way to find—"

Sure enough, the three men Zack had been chasing had moved away from us and were now trying to hide behind a small grove of thin, leafless trees. Through the branches, I could clearly see that the three guys were all wearing matching clothes: loose brown shirts with fringe along the bottom, brown leather pants, and some funky long stockings underneath. But everything they wore was

torn and muddy. They didn't have shoes on.

I am usually supercurious and normally I'd have stopped everything to ask about the men and their clothes, but I was going to deal with Zack first.

"You made me look like a fool in class," I told him. "I didn't have any idea who Mr. C was talking about." And just to show how mad I was, I growled at him.

Just then, Bo and Jacob caught up with us. Jacob was laughing that Zack and I were fighting. Usually he's the one who fights with Zack. "Want me to hold him down for you?" Jacob offered.

"No thanks," I said. "I want him to apologize! Zack ruined my whole day."

"We don't have time for this," Zack repeated, shivering in the snow. "If we don't talk to those guys, we'll never find—," he began, then stopped suddenly. Zack paused and took a deep breath. "I'm sorry, Abigail. Really." I could tell he was apologizing with his whole heart. "We should have never left without you."

A gust of wind blew. Goosebumps traveled up my

spine. "What about distracting me in class?" I asked, a little calmer.

"I'm sorry about that, too." I could tell he really meant it. "I thought you would enjoy a good laugh. You usually like jokes."

I reached out and helped him up. "I accept your apology." I thought about it for a second. "Listen. It's fine with me if you tell jokes sometimes, but never, ever, ever, do it during Mr. C's class again."

"Deal." Zack and I shook hands. Then he explained, "Remember, I told you that when I came out of the bathroom, Mr. C was already coming down the hallway? He gave me the time-travel cartridge and told me to hang on to it until after school. So before class I knew who we were visiting because of the little picture glued to the front of the cartridge."

Zack went on. "When I found out who we were visiting, I felt like this History Club mission was really important. You know me. Usually, when stuff is serious, I get nervous and stressed," Zack shivered, then grinned. "I decided that I'd tell jokes today instead of worrying so much."

"I think I like it better when you worry," Jacob put in. He quickly glanced at the computer and reported, "We only have an hour and fifty-three minutes until our time runs out. We don't have an extra second to spare for dopey riddles."

"There's always time for a joke. Just wait and see," Zack told his brother as he dusted the snow off his back.

"Did anyone ever tell you who we are here to see?" Bo asked me, clearly wanting to be helpful.

"I'm a pretty good detective," I said. "I figured it out by myself. It's February 16, 1778. We are in Valley Forge, Pennsylvania. And"—I smiled proudly—"we're here to find George Washington!"

The only thing I still didn't know was what George Washington was quitting. What did we need to convince him to do?

I was about to ask Bo when Zack asked, "What was GW's favorite tree?"

"GW?" I wondered.

"It's short for George Washington," Zack told me. "Come on. Guess. What was GW's favorite tree?"

Obviously Zack was going to finish his joke whether I wanted to hear it or not, so I shrugged.

"The infantry!" His belly shook as he laughed. "Infantry means soldiers in an army."

I didn't honor him with even a little giggle. The joke just wasn't funny.

"Speaking of infantry," Bo said, looking all around, "where did those three soldiers go? We should ask them where to find George Washington."

I decided to ask Bo about our mission later. It seemed more important to find the soldiers first, so I looked all around the grove of small trees. The three men weren't there anymore. I finally spotted them across the farm field. They seemed to be trying to hide behind a hay bale. Six arms and six legs were sticking out from the sides of the hay.

"What are they doing?" Jacob asked.

"No clue." Zack raised his shoulders. "Let's go find out!"

"Hopefully they know where we can find GW," Bo said, using Zack's new nickname for George Washington.

When we got close, Jacob called to the six arms, "Are you guys in the army with General George Washington?"

There was a bunch of whispering. I think they were deciding whether they should talk to us. "We used to be," the first man called out from behind the bale. His voice was nervous and shaky. One at a time, they each came out to where we could see them, but all three looked at us cautiously.

The second man surveyed the area before answering in a soft voice. "We are running away. Every day more and more soldiers desert the army. Sometimes even whole regiments, entire troops of men, run away together."

These guys were young. My sister CeCe is sixteen. I think they were about the same age. Maybe even seventeen or eighteen.

"We'd rather leave than die from cold or illness," the third guy explained. "Aren't you leaving Valley Forge too?"

Bo silently shook his head.

Zack said, "We just got here."

The guy looked surprised. "Do you have any idea what it is like in the American Continental Army?" He didn't wait for our response before saying, "We knew we would be spending the winter at Valley Forge in Pennsylvania. I thought we were going to a large military fort, but this place is a gathering of farms in a cold, bitter valley."

The first man lifted one foot to show us the bottom. It was all scarred and scabbed. "To get here we had to march miles and miles in the snow. There were not enough boots for everyone. I walked barefoot." He looked down at my feet. I felt guilty for wearing my clean, white tennis shoes.

The second man also showed us his sore foot before saying, "The British have been ruling the thirteen American colonies for too long. They are unfairly taxing us and making us follow their rules. I joined the Continental Army to help kick the British out of our land. But the British troops are strong and powerful. They have plenty of food and clothes. Our American troops are weak, and hungry, and dirty." He paused before adding, "This

Revolutionary War has been going on for two and a half years already. There is no hope. I am certain we are going to lose."

The third soldier didn't say anything. He just wrapped his hands around his belly. He was so thin, I could see the outline of his ribs through a big tear in the front of his shirt.

The boys and I fell silent. I bet we were all thinking about how hard things were for these soldiers.

After a few seconds, Jacob glanced down at the time on the computer screen and reported, "We only have an hour and forty-one minutes. Do you guys know where George Washington is?"

The first man raised his eyebrows, cautiously looking over our modern clothing. "We cannot give that information," he answered, looking really scared. He quickly grabbed his buddies and the three of them started to run up the hill, into the trees.

"Wait!" I called.

"Stop!" Zack and Jacob called out together.

But to my total surprise, it was Bo who got their attention. "We won't tell on you," Bo said calmly in a loud voice. There was something special about the bold way Bo called out to the men. He reminded me of, well, me.

The men stopped running and took a few steps back toward us. "You swear you won't report us to General Washington?" the first man asked, very seriously.

"We won't even mention you at all," Zack promised.

"We heard he is leaving Valley Forge," the third man informed us. "Talk in the camp is that he believes that he has failed."

I suddenly knew why we had come to 1778. It was our job to keep history on track and that meant that George Washington could not quit and leave Valley Forge. All of American history would change if he left.

"We have to find him immediately," I told the boys and the soldiers at the same time. "We must convince him not to leave Valley Forge."

The third man put his arm around Zack. "Good luck trying to convince him to stay. The general is a very stubborn man." He paused, then added, "And he has no sense of humor—at all." I glanced over at Zack and hoped in my heart he wouldn't try to tell George Washington any of his lame jokes.

The soldiers took turns giving us directions.

"Go past those sheep." The first man pointed at the sheep I'd seen earlier.

"Turn right at the cows," the second continued. "And go straight until you find a few tents. Beyond the tents, you will see log cabins and behind that, a stone house. That is the Pottses' home. General Washington has been using the house as headquarters."

"You best hurry if you plan to catch him before he saddles his horse, gathers his wife, and rides away," the third man finished. Then, without another word, he nodded to his buddies.

They took off up the hillside, running and ducking between trees until they were out of sight.

We hurried in the opposite direction, toward the sheep. We had to find George Washington.

I crossed my fingers that we weren't already too late.

CHAPTER FOUR

"WAS IT A RIGHT OR A LEFT AT THE COWS?" I ASKED Bo, because Bo remembers everything.

"Right at the cows, then straight past the tents," Bo informed me.

"We should keep our eyes peeled for Babs Magee," Jacob said as he hopped over a hay bale. Babs Magee was Mr. C's old apprentice, the one who stole his first time-travel computer. Now she was popping through history trying to convince people to quit.

"If George Washington is quitting, you can bet she's around here somewhere," Zack warned.

For some strange reason, probably just bad fashion sense, Babs Magee always wears a yellow coat and matching hat. "It shouldn't be too hard to find her,"

Zack added, surveying the white snow all around. "Just keep your eyes peeled for a human banana." He started to laugh. "Get it? Peeled? Banana?"

"Can you be serious for one whole minute?" I asked.

"But, Abigail," he fake whined. "I have another joke. A really good one. I swear you'll like it." We made a right turn behind a rather large, black, stinky cow. Zack patted the cow on her back. "Where's a cow's favorite place to go?"

"BLAH BLAH BLAH!" I screamed, covering my ears and running across the field toward the tents in the distance. Unfortunately, since Zack is such a fast runner, he easily caught up with me.

I had my hands over my ears, but it didn't help. I could still hear him.

"The mooovies," he said with a snort and a chuckle.

I had to admit, that one was a teeny-weeny bit funny. I would have laughed, but I didn't want to encourage him to tell another, so I held my breath until the giggle went away.

When the runaway soldier said to look for log cabins

behind a row of tents, I expected a small campsite. But what we found was more like an enormous log cabin village. There were tons of cabins. And they were pretty big. Bo told me that each one was large enough to sleep twelve soldiers.

Bo explained that some people called the camp ground at Valley Forge a log city.

"Fighting in the Revolutionary War was different from fighting wars today." Bo rubbed his chin as he recalled the facts he'd read. "When it got cold, everyone took a break. Both sides of the battle would stop, build a campsite, and hang out until spring. Then, when it got warm, they'd start fighting again. During the six months the soldiers were in Valley Forge, more than twelve thousand American soldiers, officers, and volunteers stayed here."

"Wow! That's a lot of people," Jacob exclaimed. "No wonder they called this place a city!"

"You there," a young man called to us as we walked through the camp. He was tall, with a brown mustache that bounced as he talked. "Go, gather wood. Then come stoke the fire. My soldiers are

cold." He indicated a gathering of thin, shivering soldiers standing around a fire pit. There was a tiny little fire going. It wasn't big enough to keep anyone warm.

He was acting pretty darn bossy for a guy who didn't know us at all. Who'd he think he was? I tapped myself on the chest. "Are you talking to me?"

"No," he said directly. "I am not speaking to you." He took a long look at my blue jeans and raincoat. "You are a girl, aren't you?"

I started to get upset at his question. "Of course I'm a girl. Can't you tell a boy from a girl?" I couldn't believe how rude he was. I was just getting going when I felt Bo give me a small warning kick on the side of my shoe.

"Mellow out, Abigail." Bo leaned in toward my ear and whispered, "Check out the medals on his uniform." I saw a few pinned to his shirt. His uniform wasn't nearly as torn as the clothes the runaways were wearing. "He's a commanding officer," Bo said. "He has mistaken Zack, Jacob, and me for soldiers. He thinks you are a female volunteer."

"But you and the twins aren't soldiers," I grunted. "And I'm not a volunteer."

"He doesn't know that." Bo bent his head toward a group of women nearby. "Look over there."

About ten women were gathered around a river's edge. Some were on the shore. Others had hiked up their skirts and were standing in the stream. They were doing laundry, scrubbing at soldiers' clothes with the icy water. I could see soapy bubbles floating downstream. I shivered just watching them. It must have been freezing.

"You belong with the women," the bossy commanding officer informed me. "You may either go to the laundry or to the hospital area to nurse the sick." I stared at him. "Choose," he said all tough and snotty. "That's an order."

My cheeks turned red. It's nearly impossible for me to take orders from anyone.

"We shouldn't make trouble," Bo said to us softly. "Abigail should go to the laundry. We'll quickly stoke his fire and then sneak off together."

"But—," Jacob argued. He lowered his voice so

Mr. Bossy couldn't hear us. "We have to find GW."

"It'll be okay," Bo said softly. He turned to me. "Abigail, go on. Maybe the women know where to find GW. Zack, Jacob, and I will check around here. By the time we come get you in a few minutes, we'll know exactly where we are headed. That way, we won't waste any time at all."

"I'm not being left behind again!" I put my hands on my hips and refused to move.

Jacob rolled his eyes at me. Zack sighed. And Bo shook his head. "We aren't going to leave you," they said almost at the exact same time.

The mustached officer pointed at the rock-circled fire pit. In a booming voice he gave more orders to the boys. "Collect as many large pieces of wood as you can carry. This fire needs to grow."

I decided that doing laundry had to be better than lugging wood for the fire. "Have fun getting wood," I said with half a smile. "Try not to get any splinters."

Zack must not have had any good firewood jokes, because as I turned toward the river, I could hear him mumbling and grumbling behind me.

Slowly I walked toward the women, the ice-cold river and the smelly laundry. "So," I said as I approached an older woman on the riverbank, "have you seen General Washington today?"

The woman ignored my question. Instead she asked if I had come to help.

"No," I began, but then decided to take Bo's advice. I shouldn't make trouble. And when I thought about it, as horrible as doing the laundry was, it was really important. Without these women, the soldiers couldn't do their part in the war.

In our time, women fight side by side with men. Everyone does laundry. But during the Revolutionary War, the women had jobs of their own. I felt like if I helped, even just for a minute, I'd be doing a small part toward winning the war and making America free.

"I'm here to volunteer," I said positively. I hoped she wouldn't suggest I jump in the river to wash clothes. Brrr. I shook at the thought of freezing my toes off. There had to be another job.

I was relieved when she said, "You can help Martha

with the sewing." She pointed at a distinguished-looking woman about the same age as my mom.

Martha wore a thick white cape. Her white hair was piled high on her head. There was a small light-weight bonnet pulled down over all that hair. She was sitting on a rock by the water's edge, mending clothes with a needle and thread.

As I approached, I realized that this woman looked very familiar.

When I suddenly figured out who she was, I was so excited that I quickly spun around to find the boys. But they must have still been out looking for firewood. I couldn't see them anywhere.

As hard as it is for me to wait, I'd have to be patient for them to come back.

I had good news. Great news.

I'd found Martha Washington.

CHAPTER FIVE

GW

"Mrs. Washington," I approached cautiously. I was surprisingly nervous. Sure, we'd met other famous Americans on our time-travel adventures, but this was Martha Washington!

"Come, come, girl." She waved to me with her mending still in her hand. "Choose a sock and begin to darn. Our brave soldiers need these clothes to help them stay warm."

I didn't know how to darn a sock. I could barely sew. Once my mom had shown me how to put on a button, but this was different. There aren't any buttons on socks.

I took a sock out of a basket near Mrs. Washington's

feet. It was clean, but stained gray. There were six big holes in it.

Mrs. Washington could easily tell I didn't know what to do. Using the sock she was working on, she quickly taught me how to thread the needle and make a stitch. I knew I didn't have much time, but again, I felt like what I was doing was important, so I paid careful attention. Some soldier would have one warm foot tonight thanks to me!

My stitches were horrible. Crooked and too big. Even so, I managed to close one hole and began to work on the second.

"So, how long have you been in Valley Forge?" I asked Mrs. Washington. I was really curious to learn more about her. Since the boys were still off gathering wood, I had a few extra minutes to chat.

"I arrived a little before George's birthday. We had a small party for his forty-fifth year, but with food in such short supply, there was little to eat." She sighed. "Life here is much more difficult than we ever imagined.

"Did you know," Mrs. Washington asked me, "that

George takes no pay for his work in the Continental Army? The soldiers get paid. The officers, too. But not my George. He pays for everything himself with the hope that he will be paid back after America is truly its own country."

I didn't know that. "George Washington will long be remembered for the good work he does," I said, afraid to tell too much about the future. "You'll be remembered too."

"There is nothing special about me," Mrs. Washington noted as she finished the sock she was working on and looked over at my stitches. "Tuck them a bit smaller," she advised. I thought about telling her that she was going to be the first first lady of America, but knew down deep she wouldn't believe me. So I simply nodded and got to work on the last big tear instead.

When I was finished with the sock, I put it down and asked, "Where is the general now?"

Mrs. Washington took her time replying, glancing over my shoulder at the soldiers gathered around that pitiful fire, trying to keep warm. Apparently

Jacob, Zack, and Bo hadn't returned with firewood yet.

"We live in Virginia," she told me, not answering my question at all. I knew a little about George Washington's home. It was called Mount Vernon.

Martha turned her head back from the cold, starving soldiers and said, "We have over eight thousand acres of farm land. A stable, a greenhouse, a smokehouse, a wash house, and a mansion. Nearly three hundred people work at our home. It is a gentleman's life." She nudged the basket of socks with her booted toe. "A fine life."

She wasn't getting to the part we needed to know. We needed to find GW.

"I heard that General Washington wants to leave Valley Forge," I remarked as if it were common knowledge.

"Shhh . . ." Mrs. Washington quickly put her finger to her lips. "Do you want everyone to hear?" She moved closer to me and whispered, "So many soldiers are already deserting. If they hear George and I are going home, many more will run away.

The Continental Army will get a new leader in a few days. Someone else can handle the problems. George and I are taking Nelson and Blueskin and going back to Tarter, True Love, and Sweet Lips."

"Huh?" Had Mrs. Washington suddenly started speaking a different language?

"Nelson and Blueskin are GW's horses." The soft tone of Bo's voice came from behind me. "Tarter, True Love, and Sweet Lips are his dogs." I turned to find Bo and Jacob headed my way. Zack was out of breath, rushing up behind them. All three had wooden boards piled in their arms.

"Where'd you get all that wood?" I asked, jumping up so fast, I nearly spilled the basket of holey socks.

Bo and Jacob started to speak, but Zack caught up and answered. "On the far side of camp they are making new cabins. Unused hunks of wood are just lying around, but that's not what's important." He rushed on to say, "Wait till you all hear who I saw! I was behind a different cabin from Bo and Jacob. I was collecting boards when—"

"You stole the wood?!" I cut him off, totally surprised. "How can you burn the boards the soldiers need to make their cabins?"

"Calm down, Abigail," Zack told me. "We only took the scraps. Problem around here is that there is so little wood."

"So little of everything," Mrs. Washington put in.

I introduced Mrs. Washington to my friends. The boys were as awed to meet Martha Washington as I was, especially Bo. He got all red faced and he kept staring down at his feet.

"Abigail," Zack whispered to me while Mrs. Washington was saying hello to Jacob. "Don't you want to know who I saw?"

"Not now, Zack," I said. "We have serious business to do."

"This isn't a joke," Zack said back to me. "I saw—"

I turned away from him to face Martha Washington. "Mrs. Washington," I began. "I'm not a volunteer and the boys aren't really soldiers. The truth is we've come a long way to meet your husband."

"We need to convince him not to leave Valley Forge." Jacob shuffled the wood boards in his arms as he spoke. "The future of America depends on him."

As Jacob spoke, Zack just tapped his toe and stared at me. "Now? Can I tell you now?" he asked impatiently.

"Not yet," I said, feeling a bit frustrated with Zack. "Before we do anything else, we have to convince Martha Washington to take us to her husband."

Bo turned to me, asking, "Abigail, do you have a dollar bill in your backpack?"

"I don't think so," I replied as I pulled off my pack and checked the outside pocket. I didn't have a dollar, but I did have a quarter. I knew it would work just as well. I handed the quarter to Mrs. Washington.

"What does this mean?" She looked from Jacob to Bo to Zack to me. "The man on your medal looks like my husband, George."

"It is George Washington," Jacob explained, shifting his load of wood around some more. "We time-traveled to come here. In our time, his face is engraved on our money."

Mustering his courage, Bo added, "If George Washington quits and leaves Valley Forge, he'll never become the first president of the United States."

"What is time travel? What is a president? Where are the United States?" Martha Washington handed me back the quarter.

I opened my mouth to explain, but Zack interrupted, saying, "These boards are heavy. My arms are breaking." He paused. "Plus, I really need to tell you all who I saw down by the log cabins."

"You can tell us later." Jacob quickly cut off Zack's complaining. "We still have about sixty-two minutes left to complete our mission." Jacob nodded toward his pocket where the time-travel computer was stashed. "First let's drop off this wood so the soldiers can have a warm fire." He looked at Mrs. Washington. "After we do that, will you take us to see your husband? We can explain everything when we find him."

Martha stared at us for a long moment, then said, "It will not do any good. He is at the Pottses' house writing a letter and packing our belongings. I came down to the river to volunteer for the last time."

"Please, take us to see him." I was practically begging. I flipped the quarter in the air. George Washington's silver etched face glinted at her as the quarter spun. I caught it in my fist. "We have to try."

"Fine." She reluctantly changed her mind. "But I fear you are too late. He is firmly convinced that he should quit."

Her announcement was punctuated by the crash of Zack dropping his firewood. He barely missed my toes. "That's what I've been trying to tell all of you! Over behind the log cabins, I saw Babs Magee!"

CHAPTER SIX

The Future

"WHO IS BABS MAGEE?" MRS. WASHINGTON IMME-diately asked.

"She's this woman who tries to convince people to quit their dreams," I replied.

"She wants to be famous," Zack put in. "If George Washington leaves Valley Forge, she'll try to take over being general and then"—Zack gasped as he realized what Babs was doing—"She'll become the first president of the United States."

I wasn't sure how she planned to do it. We haven't had a woman president in our time yet. And there still aren't very many women generals, either. But knowing Babs Magee, she'd already figured out how to solve those problems. She was sneaky, not dumb.

"I wish I could figure out how to tweak the time-travel computer," Jacob muttered. "Just once, I'd like to get somewhere before she does."

"Mr. C said it's just one of those computer glitches. We have to deal with her now that we know she's here," I said.

"I cannot believe anyone convinced my George to quit," Mrs. Washington insisted. "He's a very stubborn man. No," she said firmly, "George has been thinking about going home for a long time."

"I bet she just helped him make the decision," I said. "She's tricky like that. She probably reminded him of all the reasons he should quit."

"Like no uniforms, no food, runaway soldiers, the Continental Army continually losing battles, the freezing cold, and how he has a nice house waiting for him in Virginia." Zack listed all the reasons GW might quit, then said, "Now that I am thinking about it, if I were GW, I'd quit too."

"That's nothing new." Jacob rolled his eyes. "You quit everything."

It was true. No one was as good of a quitter as

Zack. In just the past few weeks, he'd given up pottery club, math club, and Ping-Pong. Zack was still searching for his thing. . . . Sometimes I wondered if quitting might just be his thing.

"It is true that there is much work to be done at Valley Forge and much need for supplies," Mrs. Washington told Zack. "However, all those things you mention can get better. I have faith that George can turn these soldiers into a good, strong army."

She turned to all of us. "If you can convince George to stay, I am willing to stay and help as well. I've already warned you how stubborn he is. But after you speak to him, if he still wants to leave, we will go home immediately." Mrs. Washington moved a few steps ahead of us and began leading the way to the Pottses' house.

As we walked, something in the distance caught my eye. I saw a glint of yellow coat and matching hat moving between the cabins. "Is that her?" I asked the boys.

Bo took a long, hard look, and reported, "That's definitely Babs Magee. She's talking to someone." He squinted at the pair, then said, "I should have known! Babs is hanging out with Benedict Arnold."

The name Benedict Arnold sounded familiar and I asked Bo who it was.

"Benedict Arnold was a friend of George Washington's. But he became a traitor. Late in the war, he turned against the Continental Army and took sides with the British. He pretended to be on the side of America but really wasn't." Sometimes I think Bo has an entire encyclopedia stored in his brain.

"What do we do?" I felt desperate. Obviously, Babs was going to get the traitor, Benedict Arnold, to help her take over GW's life.

"I say we forget about Babs," Jacob suggested. "Let's focus on getting George Washington to stay at Valley Forge."

Bo agreed with Jacob. "If we can get him to stay, she'll fail."

"Are you sure you don't want me try to steal her time-travel computer? If I got it, she'd never be able to time travel again." Zack bent low, ready to run after her. "I could do it." He stood up a little straighter and admitted, "Well, at least I could try."

"Leave her alone," I said as we approached a large stone house. "Let's talk to GW instead. We'll get her another time." I hopped a few steps forward to catch Mrs. Washington. "Is this the Pottses' house?"

"Yes," Mrs. Washington told me. "This is the Continental Army headquarters."

Suddenly Bo pointed up at a flag hanging in front of the house. "Lucky for us, George Washington is still here."

"That flag is the commander in chief standard," Mrs. Washington explained to us. "The background is blue with sixteen large pointed stars. This flag means that George Washington is the leader of all Revolutionary War troops."

"The important thing," Bo added, "is that GW never goes anywhere without it!"

"He wouldn't leave without his horses, either," Jacob said. He pointed out two horses tied to a post. A wagon sat nearby, ready to be hitched. I didn't know which horse was Nelson or which was

Blueskin, but I hoped that in the next few minutes, both horses would be back in the Valley Forge stable, right where they belonged.

Inside the house, it was really quiet—too quiet, if you asked me. There was no sign of GW anywhere we could see.

Mrs. Washington wished us luck and told us to go on upstairs to look for her husband. She needed to get something called firecakes from the kitchen. They would eat the firecakes on their journey home. She disappeared down a hallway.

We hustled up the stairs and through the first door we saw. We were in such a hurry, we didn't think twice about barging into the room.

"Oh my gosh," I exclaimed as we entered GW's bedroom. "We should have knocked."

It was totally embarrassing. General George Washington, the father of our country, wasn't packing. He was sound asleep and snoring. But that wasn't the worst part. The worst part was that he was wearing nothing more than a thin white gown, more like a girl's dress than boy's pajamas.

GW was curled up on top of his bed covers. And on top of him were scraps of cloth paper. A quill pen lay on the bed. A blue ink jar had tipped over. Ink was smeared everywhere.

"What's he doing?" I whispered to the boys. It looked like he was in the middle of a messy art project.

"I'll check it out." Careful not to wake GW, Jacob snuck over to the bed and snatched a piece of paper off his belly. Jacob tossed it back over his shoulder to Zack.

Zack missed the catch, nearly stumbling back into a brass pot near the bed. I knew what that pot was for. It was called a chamber pot and was what people peed in on cold days when they didn't go out to the outhouse.

Luckily Zack missed the pot and Bo caught the paper. After a quick glance, Bo told us that it was part of a letter written to Governor George Clinton.

"Didn't we have a president of the United States called Clinton?" I asked the boys upon hearing the name.

"That was Bill Clinton," Bo reminded me. "He was the forty-second president. In 1778, George Clinton was Governor of New York and a good friend of GW's. When he felt most desperate, George Washington wrote Governor Clinton a letter asking if he might be able to help with necessary supplies. In this famous letter, GW asks for cattle to be driven down from New York."

In a hushed voice, Bo began to read:

"To Governor George Clinton
Head Quarters, Valley Forge,
February 16, 1778
Dear Sir: It is with great reluctance, I trouble
you on a subject, which does not fall within
your province; but it is a subject that occasions
me more distress, than I have felt, since the
commencement of the war."

Bo hummed as he skipped a little.

"I mean the present dreadful situation of

the army for want of provisions, and the
miserable prospects before us, with respect to
futurity.”

A lot of words. Big words.

"What does all that mean?" I asked the boys.

"The letter means that we do not have enough supplies," George Washington answered. I jumped at the sound of his voice.

I was surprised he didn't yell at us for being in his room, or seeing him in his nightie, or reading his mail—all things I'd have screamed about if I were him.

I quickly and quietly asked Bo. Bo said that a lot of kids volunteered to help during the Revolutionary War. He was used to having people around all the time.

"My men are freezing cold and starving to death," George Washington told us. "The new American congress has no money to send me. There are no supplies nearby because the British are taking every-thing first." He shook his head sadly. "This letter means that I have no one else to ask for help."

He picked his ink jar up off the bed and wiped off the bottle with a rag. Then he got the quill pen. George Washington put both items in a nearby open crate before closing the lid with a slam. There were many similar crates lined against the walls of the room.

"Thank you for waking me up," he told us. In a move faster than I've ever seen, he leaped behind a fabric curtain and within seconds was dressed in full military gear.

"I must leave now," he said as he headed to the bedroom door.

I was feeling bold and strong and wanted to be the first to try to convince him to stay. I stepped in front of our great American leader.

"Sir," I said, my voice loud and determined, "you can't leave. America won't be a free country unless you win the Revolutionary War. These men and women need you to lead them. Only you can keep the soldiers from deserting." I could see he didn't believe me, so I pressed on. "You must help them.

Send the letter to your friend and don't quit. You've gotta hang in there."

GW stepped around me. "Martha!" he called down the stairs. "Are the horses saddled?" I knew she probably couldn't hear him, since she had gone to the kitchen.

Before George Washington could call out again, Zack took a try. "I know all about quitting," Zack put in sincerely. "Quitting feels good at first, but sometimes you wonder why you gave up."

George Washington made a noise that sounded like "hummph." Then he called for Martha again.

The more stubborn GW acted, the more courageous Bo seemed to become. I could tell that Bo really wanted to convince GW not to quit. "You can't quit just because there aren't enough supplies," he said. "In the next few weeks, supplies will come along with a new quartermaster to help organize everything. A man named Baron Von Steuben is also on his way to help you train the troops."

George Washington turned to us. "The problem is greater than supplies and training troops. My men lost too many battles befoe we came to Valley Forge. The troops are tired. They do not think they can win." He sighed. "When you stop thinking you can win, you have already lost." Then he added, "I do not believe we can win either. Every battle I have led lately has ended in disaster."

"That isn't true," Bo said, continuing to gather his nerve to speak loudly to an adult—a really famous adult. "You had a big day when you crossed the Delaware."

"Yes," GW said, a far-off look in his eye. "That was a fine morning. We surprised the British on Christmas at dawn and drove them back. But"—he looked directly at Bo; Bo was twitching his knee nervously—"that win was over a year ago."

George Washington looked sad. "If the British attacked us here"—he moved over to the window and glanced outside—"we would be crushed. My soldiers are too weak to fight." He closed the curtains. "Before coming to Valley Forge, I had two chances to stop the British, at Brandywine and Germantown. Both times we lost the battles and had to retreat. Now my troops have no confidence in me."

"Yes, they do," I insisted, although I knew it was no use. We were talking to a defeated leader. He was quitting and nothing we could do would stop him.

Well, almost nothing. We were going to have to take him to the future!

As GW called down the stairs, "Martha! Have the men bring the horses around to the front," I quickly whispered my idea to the boys.

"We only have forty-one minutes." Jacob told us that Mr. C had added a new button to the computer that would let him change the settings as many times as he wanted. Now we could easily make multiple jumps through time if we needed to.

"Will forty-one minutes be enough?" Zack asked.

"It has to be," Bo said confidently after a little chin scratching. "Let's go."

In the blink of an eye, Jacob reset the computer and pulled out the cartridge. The glowing green hole opened in the floor of GW's bedroom.

In a flash of what I must say was brilliant planning,

I screamed, teetering over the hole as if I was about to fall in. I flailed my arms and shouted, "Help me," in my most pathetic voice.

Just like I expected, being a general and a good man, George Washington couldn't resist saving my life. He leaped forward and grabbed my hands in a single motion. Once his hands were around mine, I leaned back with all my weight. I'm not very heavy, but we were at the edge of the hole, so it worked. He lost his balance and we toppled into the time-travel hole together. The boys jumped in after.

We were headed back to the future.

CHAPTER SEVEN
Army, Navy

WE LANDED IN THE PATHWAY OF A HUGE ARMORED tank.

"Move!" Jacob shouted, grabbing my arm as the tank came barreling toward us. I leaped out of the way. So did Zack. And Bo. But when I looked back to where we had been standing, George Washington was still there.

We didn't have time to coordinate a rescue mission. All four of us jumped toward George Washington at the same time, knocking him sideways to the ground and away from the rolling tank wheels.

"Whew," Bo breathed a sigh of relief. "That was close."

"GW was almost flat as a pancake," Zack said, laying

his head back on the ground and sighing.

I quickly stood up, realizing that GW was already on his feet. He was staring after the tank. "What was that? A metal horse?" he asked, looking confused.

"It's an armored tank. Army soldiers are protected as they ride in it," Jacob explained as he dusted dirt off his pants. "We brought you to the future—I mean, to your future. It's *now* for us."

We had brought George Washington to a modern army base. When I came up with the idea of bringing him here, it was to show him how the army worked in our time, to show him how people in America still fought for the freedoms of the Declaration of Independence.

I thought that since he was a general, he'd like it, and I hoped it would inspire him to stay at Valley Forge. "When your soldiers win the Revolutionary War," I said, "America will become an independent country."

"America needs a different leader. I am going home," George Washington told us. He couldn't keep his eyes off the tank.

"America needs you," Bo said with determination. "The British will admit defeat and sign a peace treaty in 1782. They will go back to Britain. From then on, America will be independent and free. In 1787 the thirteen colonies will unite into states. Today we have fifty United States of America."

As the tank rolled farther away, I told George Washington everything I knew about the United States Army, which wasn't much. "The United States Army defends our land," I said. "They protect America and help to keep people in other countries safe too."

"Today's army does basically the same thing in our time as it did in yours," Jacob added. He also explained that similar to 1778, there are officers and infantry soldiers, and that everyone gets paid—even generals.

Suddenly we heard the sound of marching feet.

"Hup, two, three, four," a man's voice called out nearby. "Hup, two, three, four." A group of soldiers in finely polished shoes and clean, crisp uniforms marched by.

"Our modern troops are well supplied," I told George Washington, pointing out the soldiers' clothing as they passed. I thought that at least one of the soldiers would have turned to look at some guy dressed like George Washington and a bunch of kids standing in the middle of the army base, but not one man or woman glanced our way. They stared straight ahead as they passed us by with rhythmic steps.

"Interesting," George Washington said. He began to walk away, heading to where the tank had turned a corner and disappeared. "I like your army. I see that men and women soldiers are training together. Martha would also enjoy the warm climate here."

I had asked Jacob to take us to an army base in California. I was tired of being cold at Valley Forge.

"I will remember this fondly when I am resting comfortably at Mount Vernon," George Washington said over his shoulder to us. "Take me back to Valley Forge. I need to load the wagon."

I looked to Zack to see if he wanted a turn convincing GW, but he was busy thinking about something else.

"You can't quit Valley Forge," Jacob said as we all caught up with George Washington. GW had really long legs. Even though he was walking, we had to run to keep up. "You have to go back and fight for freedom so America can exist. Without you"—Jacob waved his arms around the base—"There would be none of this."

George Washington seemed to be considering Jacob's words. At least he stopped walking. It was possible that he stopped because he couldn't find the tank. No matter why, I was glad he was standing still. It was hard to convince him of anything while we were moving.

Out of the blue, Zack cheered, "I've got one!" He'd been so quiet the whole time since we'd landed. I was surprised to hear his voice. "Knock. Knock."

"Zack, now's not the time for jokes." I glanced over at GW. Bo was still being courageous. He was peppering GW with army facts.

I heard Bo say, "After you win the Revolutionary War, we'll continue to need a strong army to protect us. Today's American Army has more than four hundred thousand enlisted soldiers and seventy-six thousand officers." He was sharing statistics about the number of bases in both the United States and other countries when Zack said, "Come on, Abigail. Let me tell you a joke. You don't want me to start complaining and worrying, do you?"

Joking or whining. Hmm. I wasn't sure which Zack I liked better. I gave up and said, "Who's there?"

"Tank," Zack said with a smile.

"Tank who?" I asked.

"Tank you!" Zack said, holding his side and laughing.

I didn't laugh. "Jacob and Bo," I called out to where they stood, shaking my head at Zack's dopey joke, "this United States Army visit isn't working. Anyone got another idea?"

Bo did. Seconds later, Jacob's thumbs flew over the computer's buttons as he reprogrammed the settings. The glowing time-travel hole opened in the ground. Bo, Jacob, and I caught the father of our country off guard by shoving him into the hole together. Zack followed us in, still laughing.

A second later, we landed somewhere new.

"Batten down the hatches!" a man's voice rang out. His command echoed through the narrow chamber we'd landed in. We were crammed into the radio room on a submarine. Two chairs sat in front of a switchboard lit up with small red bulbs. We were lucky that no one else was in the room. It was a really small area.

Suddenly the submarine tilted downward and I crashed into GW.

"Where are we?" he demanded to know. "Where have you taken me?" He seemed pretty stunned, so I asked Bo to explain. It was his idea to come here, after all.

"We are on a navy submarine," Bo said, adding that the navy is the second largest branch of the United States military.

"Ah yes. Together with John Barry, John Paul Jones, John Adams, and Benjamin Franklin, I started the Continental Navy in 1775," George Washington told us. "We decided to gather together army officers and soldiers who knew something about the sea."

"The Continental Navy had about fifty ships by the end of the Revolutionary War," Bo told him. "Today, the United States Navy has about two hundred eighty-one ships and over four thousand operational airplanes." Bo pointed around at the control panels in front of us. "We are on a navy submarine."

"What is a submarine?" GW asked us. I could tell he had a lot of questions brewing. I totally admire people who are as curious as I am.

"A submarine is a special kind of boat that can travel under the water," Jacob told him.

"And what is an airplane?" he wondered.

Before I could explain what airplanes were, a woman in a blue uniform rushed into the room.

"Oh no," she gasped when she saw us. "Didn't you get off with the tour group? We are headed out to sea on a training mission!"

"It's okay," Zack said with a wink. "We can just pop out of here anytime we want. No problem."

"No problem?!" she was nearly shouting at us. "This is a huge problem. The captain will have my head when he finds out I didn't sweep the sub for civilians before descent." As she said it, the submarine tilted again. I could feel us going down lower and lower into the sea. From somewhere outside the room, I heard a man's voice call out, "Up periscope!"

The woman looked frazzled. "All right," she said, taking a deep breath. "I'll get you out of here soon enough. First I need to check the radio equipment to be sure it's working." The woman turned away from us and put on a pair of headphones. She began pressing buttons on a nearby control panel.

"Thirty-seven minutes left on the computer," Jacob announced. He looked at GW. "Pretty impressive, eh? Today we can fight battles, make sneak attacks, and protect America from under the sea."

"There are nearly half a million men and women serving in the U.S. Navy," Bo added, "all thanks to you for realizing the importance of defending our waters."

"It's time to go back to Valley Forge and stay there," I told GW. "Now do you understand why? The ideas that we love and protect came from you and your friends." I stood on tiptoe to boldly get my face closer to George Washington's. "You were already fighting when the Declaration of Independence was signed. You led the army and helped invent the navy."

"The Continental Congress will appoint another leader to lead the fight at Valley Forge!" he announced. "I want to sit in my favorite chair and warm my feet before the fire at my beloved home." GW headed over to where the woman was sitting. "But before we go," he added, "I'd like to learn more about this underwater boat." He searched for the right word, then said, "I mean, submarine." He stood behind her as she twisted dials and pressed knobs, watching her every move.

"Speaking of submarines," Zack raised his eyebrows at me, "what did the ocean say to the submarine?"

I sighed loudly. I was getting really tired of Zack and his jokes. Jacob was busy with our computer so Bo saved me and took this one. "What?" he replied.

"Nothing. It just waved!" Zack said.

It wasn't funny. Not even a tiny bit. Zack's jokes were getting worse as the day went on. I made my decision. Jacob had been right, a worried Zack was a lot better than a joke-telling one. I hoped he'd run out of jokes soon.

"I've got a new idea!" Jacob looked up from the computer and everyone turned toward him. The woman turned around too.

"I'd almost forgotten about you," she said. "I better go alert the captain. We're going to have to return to shore." She set down her headset and hurried from the room.

Without another word, Jacob pressed wildly at the computer buttons, changing the settings. The time-travel hole opened in the middle of the radio room floor.

"Where are we going now?" I asked.

"Another place to convince George Washington," Jacob said. "It's time to hit the skies!"

I thought I knew what he meant, but before I could ask, George Washington's voice boomed in the small room. "Skies? What does that mean? I insist that you take me back to Valley Forge now. I must saddle my horse and begin my journey!" He stood tall and shouted, "That's an order!" Clearly GW wasn't going to be tricked or pushed into going anywhere else.

I pinched my lips together, trying to figure out how to get GW into the hole before it closed.

"If you can't bring GW to the hole," Jacob said, frantically pushing buttons on the computer, "maybe I can bring the hole to GW." Jacob is so super-duper smart at computers. If there was a way, I knew he'd find it.

The time-travel hole was beginning to shrink. So far, none of us had leaped into it. I was starting to feel nervous, when suddenly, the hole started to move. It was slinking across the floor like a snake.

"It's working!" Zack gave his brother a big thumbs-up.

Bo slapped Jacob heartily on the back.

And a second later, the hole crept right under

George Washington, gobbling him up. I heard him shout, "No!" as he fell in.

"Way to go, Jacob!" I gave him a high five as I jumped in following GW. The boys leaped in after me.

CHAPTER EIGHT
Air Force

"GRAB YOUR PARACHUTES, AIRMEN. IT'S TIME TO go." A commanding officer in a jump suit was speaking to rows of men and women lined up on benches.

"Jacob," I cried. "Tell me you didn't bring us to—"

"Yep." Jacob smiled, showing all his teeth. "We're flying high with the United States Air Force. If seeing the air force doesn't amaze GW and convince him to stay at Valley Forge, nothing will." He looked at the computer and groaned. "We only have thirty minutes left."

We'd landed in the back of an airplane. It wasn't like any regular plane I'd taken on vacation. There were no nice cushy seats or flight attendants with drink carts. Basically it looked like the whole plane had been emptied out, leaving rows of benches and nothing else.

All the airmen on the plane were busy putting on their parachutes. I knew it wouldn't be long before someone noticed us. I quickly turned to Bo. Maybe there were some air force facts swimming around in his head that would help.

"In 1947," Bo said, "another part of the American military was created. It is called the United States Air Force." Bo was still acting pretty bold. I hoped it would last until we finally convinced GW.

GW looked blankly at Bo, but Bo went on anyway. "The air force has about 358,600 men and women serving in it. And about nine thousand airplanes."

"Airplanes?" GW asked. I'd forgotten we'd never explained about airplanes to him.

"In December 1903, two brothers invented a machine that could fly," Zack told him. I was relieved that he wasn't telling GW any airplane jokes—yet. "Since then, people have been building better and better flying machines. We call them airplanes."

"Are we in an airplane now?" George Washington

looked around. Of course he didn't know we were in an airplane. We were nowhere near a window. For all he knew, we were in a silver metal tunnel— with benches.

"We're flying very high above the ground," I replied. "As high as the clouds. The United States military got even stronger after airplanes were added. Planes can move people around the world quickly, bring supplies, and even drop bombs."

"I know bombs," George Washington said, recognizing the word. "We use those types of exploding weapons in the Revolutionary War." He sighed. "Maybe we could win the war if I had one of these flying machines. The British would be caught unawares."

Finally! He was thinking about ways to win the Revolutionary War. That was a change, even if he wanted to use airplanes to do it.

"You won't need an airplane to win the war," Bo told him.

GW nodded, considering Bo's words. We were getting even closer to convincing him!

Jacob checked the computer and warned us, "Twenty-five minutes." Then he asked GW, "Are you ready to go back to Valley Forge and prepare to fight?"

George Washington paused. I could see he was really thinking about everything we'd said and what we'd shown him.

"Don't forget about the rights that your friends wrote about in the Declaration of Independence: life, liberty, and the pursuit of happiness." Bo was giving it one last try. "Everything we know in our world depends on you going back to Valley Forge and leading the battles to guarantee us those rights."

"It's why you are known as the father of our country!" I put in, crossing my fingers that we'd finally convinced him.

"The father of your country?" GW shook his head. "I do not understand."

"It's what everyone in the future will call you." I was ready to drop to my knees and start begging. "You have to go back to Valley Forge and stay there."

George Washington looked at me carefully. I swear I could see a change in his eyes. Maybe we'd gotten through to him at last? Martha was right. He sure was stubborn.

George Washington opened his mouth to speak when suddenly the air force officer at the front of the plane called to him. "You there, grab your parachute. It's time to go."

GW strode to the front of the plane saying, "I am struggling to decide between retiring to my comfortable home in Virginia or remaining in the unpleasantness of Valley Forge. Where else am I meant to be going?"

"If you're on my plane," the officer said, "you'll be going out there." And with that he pointed out the open door of the plane. We'd been talking so much, I hadn't noticed that the plane was now empty. All the airmen had parachuted away.

The officer handed GW a parachute, and quickly reviewed how to put it on and open it. To my amazement, GW did as he was told without argument. What was he thinking?!

Bo, Jacob, Zack, and I hurried forward to prevent GW from jumping.

The man led GW to the door. "Bend your knees and jump," he advised. Then, as an afterthought, added, "Your uniform is not regulation. See the supply officer on base when we get back."

"I will have you know," GW said as he bent his knees, "I designed this uniform myself." And with that, the father of our country leaped out of the plane.

"Oh no!" I shrieked. It had all happened so fast, we didn't have enough time to stop him.

"I know what to do." Zack quickly shared his idea with Jacob. "Hurry."

We rushed to the door of the plane.

"I don't know how you children got on board," the officer told us, "but parachuting is for airmen only. You'll ride to the airport with the pilot. We'll make arrangements for you to be returned to your parents from there."

"No need," Jacob said, frantically stabbing at buttons on the computer before slipping in the

cartridge. Turning to us, Jacob warned, "Jump carefully. You gotta aim your feet toward the center of the time-travel hole."

Out the door of the plane, I could see the glowing hole shimmering just below George Washington. With his parachute open, he glided gently down through the smoke.

"This is crazy," Zack said. "I'm about to jump out of a speeding plane without a parachute. But am I complaining? No." He grinned as he bent his knees, preparing to leap. "What did Geronimo say when he jumped out of the airplane?" he asked.

"I have no idea," I said, taking his hand in mine. I was way too scared to jump alone.

"Me!" he cried out as we jumped together.

The last thing I heard as I fell through the time-travel hole was the air force officer shouting at Bo and Jacob with great concern. "You kids don't have parachutes!"

Jacob replied, "Thanks, but we don't need them!"

CHAPTER NINE

Marines

WHEN WE LANDED, THE PARACHUTE WAS COVERing George Washington's whole body like a ghost costume. He was wiggling underneath to take it off. Jacob and Zack moved in to help.

Once GW's head was out and he saw us standing there, his face turned red. "I see that we are not yet at Valley Forge," he said angrily.

"We can't take you there until we are certain you won't leave for Mount Vernon," I replied.

"We have to make sure history is back on track," Jacob said, peeling the rest of the parachute off George Washington and tossing it aside.

We'd landed in a large field. It was cold outside and reminded me a great deal of Valley Forge. There

wasn't much around, only a few rolling hills and some sparse trees. In the distance, I could see houses and buildings, not log cabins, but the feel of a small military city was familiar.

The sound of gunfire nearby startled me. It came from over a small hill behind us.

I turned quickly around. Jacob was already climbing the hill. "Hey," he called back to us. "There's a sign up here that says this is a shooting range for the United States Marines."

We hustled up the hill to see. Even though he was mad, George Washington seemed eager to investigate.

"I know the Marines," GW said as he crested the hill. "We created the Continental Marines in 1775 for ship-to-ship fighting. They also managed shipboard security and helped landing forces."

"Today," Bo got started on his factarama, "the marines do more than that. They are a special division of the United States military that operates on land, sea, and even in the air."

"Do they have airplanes?" George Washington asked.

When Bo said yes, GW seemed a bit less angry that we weren't back in 1778. "They also have boats and submarines. The marines have tanks, too," Bo added.

As Bo said it, I realized that we probably could have made one stop instead of four. I crossed my finger that this last place would be the one to finally convince GW.

"We only have nineteen minutes," Jacob warned as Bo geared up for more facts.

"More than two hundred ninety thousand people currently serve in the United States Marines," Bo reported. GW was looking more and more interested by the second.

I was suddenly curious. If the marines did everything all the other branches of the military did, what made them special? I asked Bo, figuring that GW would want to know as well.

"The marines work at the direct command of the president," Bo replied. "If the president wants to send troops somewhere quickly, he uses the marines. Some people even call the marines the President's Own."

"Hmm," George Washington mumbled as he moved down the hill. The *rat-a-tat-tat* of more gunfire sounded. This time it was clearly off to our left. We found a path and followed it. The path was designed so that no one would get accidentally shot as they visited the shooting range.

"Which president is it that commands these men?" George Washington asked as the men and women of the United States Marines came into view.

Jacob responded, "The president of the United States."

We'd reached the marines. From the safety of the path, we could see men and women lying on the ground, shooting at targets in the distance. They shuffled forward on their bellies, aimed with a rifle, and shot at a bull's-eye in the middle of a round wooden disk.

An officer was commanding them when to scootch forward and when to shoot.

It was very exciting to watch. I could have stayed there all day. These troops were training for battle. Where the battle was, or where it might be in the future, I had no idea. But these men and women were going out into the world to protect the freedoms we'd been talking about with GW all day.

That reminded me. I couldn't stand here watching our military train all day. We had to convince GW to go back to 1778! He had to unpack his crates.

"You will be the first president," I told George Washington proudly.

"I will not," he replied. He was awed by the way these troops trained. By the way his eyes were squinted and his jaw clenched, I could tell he was studying their movements as a general.

"Even if the Continental Army won the Revolutionary War, there are no plans for a president. People are talking about an American King." Though he was standing, George Washington was moving his shoulders back and forth similar to the way the marines were doing it on the ground.

"When you are elected in 1789," Bo put in, "no one will agree to having a king. You'll be called the president of the United States."

The marines were no longer crawling and shooting.

They had changed to a different drill, in which they ran, stopped, dropped to the ground, aimed, and shot their weapon. It was another way they could protect America and Americans.

George Washington was interested in these new moves, too. "I will never be president. At most I will remain commander in chief of the armies of the United States."

Zack immediately turned to me. "Did he say he *will* remain commander in chief?" Zack looked so excited.

We nearly had him. I was sure of it.

I gave Bo a pat on the back and said, "Bring it home, baby. He's yours now."

It was a lot of pressure for a shy guy, but Bo'd been doing so great all day. I was sure he could wrap things up.

"Make it quick," Jacob said with a supportive grin. "We've got twelve minutes and the clock is ticking." We'd never gone over our time before. We were sure something horrible would happen if we did. And we didn't want to know what that was—ever.

Bo took a deep breath and quickly said, "After the

drafting of the United States Constitution in 1787, the commander in chief and the president of the United States will become one and the same. You'll be the only president voted to office unanimously by the entire electoral college."

I knew something to add! I was thrilled to be able to contribute. "And," I said, "you'll give a really short inaugural address." I smiled. "But your second one will be even shorter."

All that anger I'd seen in GW's face was gone. He looked at us, asking, "And by becoming president of the United States, I'll command all the different military branches we have seen today? The army, navy, air force, and marines?" He took another look at the soldiers. Not one man or woman had missed a target the entire time we'd been watching. These troops were hot!

"Not the air force," Zack reminded him.

"Oh, yes," GW responded. "I nearly forgot airplanes were not invented in 1778. Perhaps I should explore the idea of creating an airplane in my time. It would certainly be helpful."

"Please don't ruin history for the Wright Brothers," I said. "They deserve their place too."

"It seems we all have a place in history," GW told us. "I understand why I should go back to 1778, send the letter to my friend, procure supplies, and train my troops." He paused. "My troops must win the Revolutionary War. I see now that freedom is important for all generations. If I don't fight for it in mine, there will be no one to fight for it in yours."

It was a great speech. Short, too. George Washington really knew how to pack a punch with very few words.

"If you're ready, then, let's go," Jacob said, and was about to put the cartridge into the back of the computer when GW interrupted.

"Wait!" GW commanded. As he said it, my heart started to race. I didn't want him to have changed his mind about staying again. We didn't have time for that.

"War is serious business," George Washington told us. "And although I am a serious man, I have come to enjoy the merriment, jokes, and mirth of your time." I thought this was strange, since GW hadn't cracked a smile all day. Maybe he had been smiling on the inside.

"I will make you a deal," GW said. "If you give me one moment of laughter I will once again bow my head to the strains of Valley Forge." He crossed his arms over his chest and waited.

Zack went first. He quickly repeated all the jokes he'd been annoying us with.

GW just stared at him. No laughs. Not even a mini giggle. There was no sign that he was smiling on the inside, either. "I can't think of any new ones," Zack admitted at last. "I'm all out."

"Thank goodness," Jacob said with a sigh of relief. Jacob knew a bunch of jokes about computers but decided not to tell them. Explaining what computers are would just take way too much time.

Bo simply shrugged. He'd worked hard today. He was pooped out and back to being supershy.

It was up to me. One good joke and we'd be headed back to Valley Forge. I needed one that General

George Washington would understand. A funny one. One that would prove a point.

I got it.

"What kind of tea did the American colonists thirst for?" I asked the father of our country.

"I do not know," George Washington replied.

"Liberty." I smiled at George Washington, knowing, like the marines, I'd given it my best shot.

And then it happened. GW began to smile. It started slow at first. Just a chuckle. A little shake in his chest. Then, finally, with only eight minutes left on the computer's clock, GW laughed.

Jacob didn't waste even a second more. At the sound of GW's first snicker, he slipped the cartridge into the back of the computer and opened the green hole.

GW ruffled my hair and smiled. "Well done, my children," he said, and all on his own, he jumped through time.

Bo, Jacob, Zack, and I held hands.

On the count of three, we jumped.

And on four we landed, because time travel is really fast.

CHAPTER TEN

February 16, 1778

WE LANDED OUTSIDE THE FRONT DOOR OF GEORGE Washington's headquarters at Valley Forge.

"Oh, there you are," Martha Washington said as she stuck her head out from behind the horse-drawn carriage. "Everything is prepared to go, just as you desired."

The wagon was hooked to the horses. I walked around to the back of the wagon and sure enough, the wooden crates we'd seen in GW's bedroom were neatly stacked inside. They were totally packed up for their departure back to Mount Vernon.

"Very good," GW told his wife, looking distracted.

Good?! It was good that she was ready to go?! What did he mean? I hoped GW hadn't changed his mind again about going back to Virginia.

He turned to Jacob, asking, "I have come to understand that you do not have very much time left on your fancy time-traveling machine. You have been announcing the minutes regularly." He nodded toward the computer in Jacob's hand. "How much time do you have remaining?"

"Six minutes," Jacob reported after a quick check.

"Can you linger for five?" GW asked us.

"We can stay for five minutes fifty-nine seconds if we need to," Jacob reported.

"No we can't," Zack groaned. "We don't know what happens if we run out of time. We could be stuck here. We might be trapped in 1778. We might never get home."

I began to laugh. "You really did run out of jokes!" I cheered.

Jacob put an arm around his brother, saying, "It's nice to hear you worry."

Bo simply smiled. It seemed that Zack wasn't the only one who'd gone back to normal. Bo'd worn himself out talking so much. He'd spent all his courage for one day. I watched him swish his foot back and forth in the snow, acting shy, just like normal.

"Please stay for a brief part of your precious time." George Washington began to take long strides toward the front door of the house. "There is something I need to do."

"We'll be here," Jacob said, carefully keeping one eye on the computer clock.

"Would you like a firecake while you wait?" Martha Washington took out a wrapped package from the wagon.

"What's firecake?" I was curious. It sounded like a weapon.

She brought out a small biscuit. It looked more like a tortilla than a muffin. The edges were burnt.

"This is what our soldiers eat when there is nothing else. It is made of flour and water. We cook it on a fire," she pointed to the burnt parts. "No one enjoys them, but often there is nothing else." She handed us each one. "I had them made to eat along our journey home."

Zack was the first to taste it. "Ewww," he said, spitting the firecake out in the snow.

I was curious so I took a bite too. It tasted like burnt toast.

Jacob and Bo weren't as brave. They both thanked Mrs. Washington and put the firecake into their coat pockets saying they weren't hungry.

"Four minutes," Jacob reported.

"Where is he?" Zack whined. "We can't just stand around here. We'll be late!" I simply rolled my eyes at him, and smiled.

Just then, George Washington came back out of the house. "Have the men unpack the wagons. We are staying at Valley Forge," he told Mrs. Washington. "These children have shown me how important it is to carry on the fight for liberty." He winked at me. "Yours was a very good joke, Abigail. I will be certain to share it with Martha this evening. She is not as serious as I am."

George Washington asked Bo, "You said we would soon receive help and supplies. Do you know exactly when?"

Bo continued to look down, shuffling his foot. "A few weeks," Bo said softly. "Baron Von Steuben is coming from France to help train the men. He will be arriving February twenty-third. The new quartermaster, a man named Nathanael Greene, will arrive on March second."

GW nodded. "I look forward to their arrival." He handed a piece of cloth paper to Bo. "I needed an extra minute to find the proper supplies. I had packed away my ink and quill. Luckily, I knew where to find replacements."

Bo held the paper for us all to see. It was the letter to Governor Clinton. George Washington had finished it and signed it. And it was ready to send.

"You there," George Washington called to a nearby soldier. "Post this letter for me."

After the soldier took the letter and walked away, George Washington said, "History is the way it should be. Thank you for showing me my role in the future of America." He smiled broadly and shook our hands one at a time.

Just as we were about to leave, the man we had

seen talking with Babs Magee showed up. George Washington introduced us to his friend, Benedict Arnold.

"I hear you are leaving Valley Forge," Benedict Arnold told GW.

I glanced around for Babs Magee. She had to be lurking around somewhere, watching, to make sure George Washington left. I was betting she was ready to move into the Pottses' House the instant the wagon pulled away. Benedict Arnold took his time surveying the wagon. He rubbed one of the horses on its nose. "Have a safe trip home. You will be missed." He didn't sound very sincere.

"Should we warn GW that his friend will become a traitor?" Zack whispered.

"Nah," Jacob held up the computer. "And forget about Babs Magee, too. As long as GW stays at Valley Forge, history is back on track. George Washington is way too stubborn to ever change his mind again."

"Benedict Arnold will get kicked out of the United States anyway," Bo put in. "After the war, he is forced to move to London. When he dies, he's poor and lonely."

"I hope he takes Babs with him," I said, knowing that she was probably waiting to hear from Benedict Arnold. And when she found out George Washington was staying, she'd be gone, off to convince the next person on Mr. C's list to quit. Of course, we'd be right behind her!

We said good-bye to George and Martha Washington and moved to a private place. Jacob pulled out the computer cartridge and the green time-travel hole opened in the frosty ground.

We were about to jump through time when voices called to us from the distance. I looked up. The three soldiers we'd seen earlier were headed our way.

"We have returned!" the first man shouted. I was glad that they weren't close enough to see the green hole. There were a lot of trees between us and them.

"We have decided to continue to fight for America's independence," the second man cried out to us.

"We hear George Washington is staying at Valley

Forge!" There was excitement in the third man's voice.

We waved at them, happy to see that they weren't deserting after all.

"Our work here is done!" I said, a huge smile on my face. I was proud that American history was once more on track. We'd done it with six seconds to spare.

The boys and I held hands, forming a small, tight circle.

And happily, we jumped home.

A Letter to Our Readers

Dear Readers,

Washington's War is a mixture of fact and fiction.

The fiction parts are the things that we made up, like four time-traveling kids. Jacob, Zack, Bo, and Abigail might remind you of kids you know, but they really exist only on the pages of our books.

However, there are many true facts about George Washington in this book. During the Revolutionary War, George Washington really did march his troops through the bitter snow to spend the winter at Valley Forge, Pennsylvania.

His soldiers didn't have warm clothes to wear or enough food to eat. The soldiers would eat firecake, but that wasn't enough to keep men healthy. Many became sick. Others would run away. Female volunteers helped around camp as best as they could, but George Washington worried that if the British attacked Valley Forge, they would lose the war.

On February 16, 1788, George Washington sent a letter to his friend Governor George Clinton in New York. He complained about the terrible conditions at Valley Forge and asked his friend to send cows, for meat and milk. A short time later, the Continental Army sent help in the form of a new supply chief, called a quartermaster, and a man to help train troops, named Baron Von Steuben.

A ragtag group of men went into Valley Forge. Six months later they were a fighting army, prepared to win the Revolutionary War and make America free.

One last thing. While writing this book, we discovered a lot of funny jokes for Zack to tell. Here is one more:

Why do pictures and statues of George Washington always show him standing?

Because he would never lie.

Have a Blast!

Stacia and Rhody

P.S. Watch for Abigail, Jacob, Zack, and Bo's next time-travel adventure, when they visit Betsy Ross!

George Washington at Valley Forge
In this painting, by William B. T. Trego, George
Washington is inspecting the troops as they head

toward Valley Forge. Created in 1883, this painting was made for a contest at the Pennsylvania Academy of Fine Arts.

Recipe for Firecake

SOLDIERS DURING THE REVOLUTIONARY WAR ATE firecake when there wasn't very much food available. Firecake is a mixture of flour and water. The soldiers would add a little salt to flavor it, if they had any. If you make it right, the firecake will be hard, flat like a pancake and taste, well, you'll have to find that out for yourself.

To make 8 firecakes:
3 cups unsifted unbleached all-purpose
 flour
1 cup water

Preheat oven to 450 degrees F.

Place the flour in a bowl and slowly add the water, kneading the dough with your hands until it is firm. Divide dough into eight equal pieces. Flatten each piece into a circle the size of your hand.

Place on a cookie sheet lined with parchment paper or foil. Bake for six minutes on one side, then turn over and bake for another six minutes.

You can burn them slightly if you want to make them exactly like the firecakes eaten at Valley Forge.

Enjoy. Or not.

Read all the books in the

Blast to the Past® series!

#1 Lincoln's Legacy

#2 Disney's Dream

#3 Bell's Breakthrough

#4 King's Courage

#5 Sacagawea's Strength

#6 Ben Franklin's Fame

#7 Washington's War

Coming Soon:

#8 Betsy Ross's Star